For Matilda, Tessa and Olivia,
storytellers and treehouse dwellers.

First American Edition 2016
Kane Miller, A Division of EDC Publishing

Text copyright © 2014 Sally Rippin
Illustrations copyright © 2014 Aki Fukuoka
Series design copyright © 2014 Hardie Grant Egmont

First published in Australia by Hardie Grant Egmont

For information contact:
Kane Miller, A Division of EDC Publishing
P.O. Box 470663
Tulsa, OK 74147-0663
www.kanemiller.com
www.edcpub.com
www.usbornebooksandmore.com

Library of Congress Control Number: 2015938844

Printed and bound in the United States of America
5 6 7 8 9 10
ISBN: 978-1-61067-464-5

Treasure Hunt

By Sally Rippin

Kane Miller
A DIVISION OF EDC PUBLISHING

Chapter One

Billie B. Brown and the rest of the Secret Mystery Club huddle in their tree house headquarters in Billie's backyard. Outside it is raining, but the four of them are cozy and warm, munching on banana muffins and sipping homemade lemonade.

Billie has her secret notebook open and her sparkly pens beside her, ready to take notes. The four of them chat **excitedly** about the new mystery they have to solve.

"A secret time capsule at school! So cool," Billie mumbles, her mouth full of muffin.

"I know!" says Jack. "Where do you think it's hidden?"

"I reckon it's buried underground," Alex says. "They're usually buried underground."

"It could be in the walls," says Mika, shrugging. "I saw a movie once like that."

"Nah," says Alex. "No one would ever find it if it was in the walls."

"I can't believe Mrs. Singh has asked for our help to find it," Billie says proudly, brushing crumbs off her lap. "This has got to be our biggest mystery ever!"

It has been two whole days since Mrs. Singh asked them to find the time capsule.

This is the first time they have all been free to come over to Billie's house after school. Billie is bursting with excitement.

"But remember, she said it was top secret!" Jack reminds her. "We can't let anyone else know. She wants it to be a surprise. And anyway, we don't want other kids to start looking for it, too!"

Billie **shudders**. *Imagine if someone else found the time capsule before us,* she thinks. *That would be awful!*

"We all have to swear to keep this top secret!" Billie says, sticking her hand out.

The other three slap their hands on top of Billie's and shout, "Cock-a-doodle-dooooo!" Then they laugh, like they do every time they shout their silly secret call.

Billie picks up her notebook and writes at the top of the page:

Secret Mystery Number Six: Where is the school's time capsule hidden?

Then she decorates the page with lots of question marks.

"So, what's our plan?" she asks the others.

The four of them sit silently for a while. Outside, the rain is starting to clear. They hear the **drip, drip, dripping** of the raindrops on the leaves.

"I know!" says Jack, sitting upright. "My uncle has a metal detector. We could ask to borrow it.

It might pick up something hidden underground."

"Great idea!" says Billie.

"Hold on," Alex frowns. "How do we explain why we are walking around with a metal detector?"

Mika grins. She reaches back and undoes the clasp of her silver necklace with the bird pendant hanging from it. It slithers into her palm. "I lost my most precious necklace at school!" she says, her eyes sparkling mischievously.

"It was given to me by my grandmother in Japan. I have to find it!"

Billie and the others giggle.

"Perfect, Mika!" Billie says.
She can't wait to get started.

Chapter Two

That evening while Billie and her family are having dinner, there's a knock on the back door.

"I'll go!" says Billie. "It'll be Jack."

Billie's mom nods. Jack is the only visitor who comes to the back door.

Billie opens the door and grins when she sees Jack standing on the back step.

"Hi, Jack!" Billie's mom calls.

"Hi!" Jack calls back. Then he whispers to Billie, "Can you come outside for a second? I've got something to show you."

"Sure!" says Billie, feeling her tummy **flip** excitedly. "What is it?"

Jack leads Billie outside. It is already dark.

In the shadows, Billie sees something leaning against the back wall.

"The metal detector!" Billie squeals. "How did you get it so quickly?"

Jack grins. "I told my dad that Mika lost her necklace in the playground and needs to find it before her mom notices it's gone. So Dad called Uncle George, who brought it over just now."

Billie sees Jack's cheeks turn a little pink. "I hope it's OK that I told them the made-up story?" he asks.

"Detectives have to do that sometimes," Billie assures him. "Especially when they're working undercover. It's not exactly lying. It's just not telling the whole truth."

Jack looks **relieved**. "Should we take it to school tomorrow? There won't be anyone there on a Saturday."

"Good idea!" says Billie. "I'll call Alex and Mika after dinner and tell them to meet us there. Eet-may ou-yay at-ay ool-skay at-ay en-tay."

Jack scrunches up his brow. "What?"

"Meet you at school at ten!" Billie giggles. "It's pig Latin. Dad taught it to me. He used to use it when he was a kid. I'll teach you guys tomorrow. It's perfect for detectives."

"Billie!" calls her dad from inside. "Your dinner's getting cold."

"Coming!" Billie calls back. "See you tomorrow, Jack!"

She does an excited little skip to the back door. *This is the best mystery ever!* she thinks happily.

Chapter Three

The next day, the four members of the Secret Mystery Club meet at the school gate at ten.

Jack has brought the metal detector with him and he shows it to Mika and Alex proudly.

"It's so cool!" Alex says. "I've always wanted one of these."

Jack smiles. "Usually my uncle only lets me use it when he's watching. But I guess he thinks I'm old enough to look after it now."

They swing open the gate and walk into the school grounds. It feels strangely quiet and the playground looks **bigger** now that it's not filled with kids.

The only people around are a little kid and his dad, bouncing a tennis ball, and a mom sitting next to a toddler in the sandbox.

Anyone is allowed to use the school grounds on weekends, but not many people do because there is a big park nearby.

"Where should we start?" Billie asks, looking around.

"I say we start on the field and work our way across the whole playground," Alex says. "It could be buried anywhere!"

The others agree.

Jack switches on the metal detector and swings it in front of him as the four of them walk slowly across the grassy field.

The detector makes a fuzzy crackling sound as it **beep, beep, beeps**.

Every now and then the beeping gets louder and faster and the four of them crouch down excitedly to see what the metal detector has found.

After an hour they have found five bottle caps, three paper clips, an earring and four coins. But no time capsule. The metal detector was lots of fun at first, but now they are getting tired from walking so slowly. And they have barely done half the field!

"Let's take a break," Billie suggests.

"Good idea," says Jack. "My arms are getting tired."

"I can hold it for a bit if you want?" Alex says.

Jack shakes his head. "I told my uncle I wouldn't let anyone else touch it."

"Let's sit under the pepper tree," Mika says. "Mom put some snacks in my bag."

"Yay!" says Billie. She loves Mika's mom's snacks. "I'm going to get a drink at the fountain. I'll meet you at the tree."

She jogs to the fountain and leans over to take a big drink of water.

When she looks up again, someone is standing right beside her. She jumps in surprise.

Billie recognizes the girl from another class but doesn't know her name.

"What are you doing with the metal detector?" the girl asks. She twirls her messy blonde ponytail between her fingers.

Billie gulps her water down. Her mind spins. "Um, my friend lost her necklace," she says, remembering their cover story just in time.

The girl nods. "What does it look like?"

Billie shifts uncomfortably from one foot to another.

She glances over to the pepper tree and sees the others sitting in the shade, eating snacks.

"It's just … um, a bird on a silver chain," she says, remembering the necklace Mika was wearing the day before.

"Are you sure it's a necklace you're looking for?" the girl says.

"Of course I am!" Billie says, feeling **flustered**. The way this girl is staring at her is making her uncomfortable.

The girl nods slowly, not taking her eyes off Billie. "A bird on a silver chain. OK. If I see it I'll let you know." She pauses. "You're Billie, right? You're in Rebecca's class."

Billie nods.

"I'm Edwina," the girl says. "I live across from the school. If I find the necklace, I'll let you know."

Billie nods again. "OK, thanks, Edwina. I'm going to go back to my friends now."

"Wait!" Edwina calls.

Billie spins around. Edwina fixes Billie with her hazel-green eyes again. "If it's something else you're looking for, I might be able to help. I know a lot about this school," she says, smiling mysteriously.

Billie doesn't even answer. She races back to the others, her heart beating loudly in her ears.

Chapter Four

Billie arrives at the tree, out of breath. "Guys!" she says, panting. "We're being spied on!"

"What?" says Mika. "But we're the spies!"

"Detectives," Alex corrects.

Billie turns around to look at the water fountain. Edwina has disappeared.

"Who's spying on us?" asks Jack.

Billie lowers her voice. "It's Edwina from Olivia's class. She lives across the street and has been watching us all this time!"

Mika gasps.

"We have to be careful!" Alex says. "What if she suspects what we're doing?"

Billie draws her friends in closer.

"I think she's already **suspicious**. When I told her the story about Mika's missing necklace, she didn't seem like she believed me at all!"

"You'd better teach us that language, Billie," Jack says. "So we can talk in front of other people without them understanding."

"What language?" Mika asks.

"Pig Latin," says Billie. "It's a made-up language my dad taught me. He said he and his friends used to use it when they were our age."

"How do you speak it?" asks Jack.

"You take a word, then move the letters that come before the vowel to the end of the word and add ay," Billie explains. "So, for example, rock would become ock-ray. Tree would become ee-tray. Dirt would become irt-day. Do you get it?"

"I think so…" Alex says. "But what if a word starts with a vowel? Like my name."

"Then you just add ay to it," Billie

explains. "So you would become Alex-ay!"

Mika grins. "Our-ay ew-nay op-tay ecret-say anguage-lay!"

"You got it!" Billie laughs.

"What did she say?" Jack frowns.

"Our new top secret language!" Billie and Mika say together, grinning.

Jack smiles. Then he sticks his hand out, palm facing down.

He scrunches up his face for a second, then crows slowly, "Ock-a-doodle-doo-cay!"

Billie slaps her hand on Jack's. Then Mika and Alex **slap** their hands down, too. "Ock-a-doodle-doo-cay!" they crow together.

Billie laughs loudly, pleased her friends like their new secret language. But then she sees a funny look pass over Mika's face.

"Did you hear that?" Mika says in a hushed voice.

"Yes, I heard something, too!"
says Jack. "From behind the tree!
A rustling sound."

All four of them fall quiet as they hear
the sound of **footsteps** running away.

Billie quickly peeks around the
wide trunk of the old pepper tree.
She is just in time to catch a blonde
ponytail disappearing behind the
school building. "Oh no!" she gasps.
"Edwina the spy!"

Chapter Five

After a long day of metal detecting,

the four members of the Secret

Mystery Club go home with

nothing but a handful of coins

each. They are still no closer to

finding the hidden time capsule.

Billie is of course disappointed about not finding it, but at the moment she is more worried about what to do about Edwina.

That night in the bath, Billie keeps thinking about the strange thing Edwina said to her by the drinking fountain. *Does she know more than she's telling me?* Billie worries. *What if she's hunting for the time capsule, too?*

Billie **squeezes** her eyes shut, takes a deep breath and lies back under the water.

She can hear bubbles gurgling up to the surface of the water as she slowly lets her breath out.

If I were hiding a time capsule in a school, where would I put it? she wonders.

She lets out her last little breath of air and sits up again. When she opens her eyes, Noah is standing next to the bath in his underpants. He has his yellow rubber duck in his hands.

"My turn!" he says. "My turn for bath now!"

Billie grins and dabs some bath foam on his nose. "OK, Nozy, I'm getting out now. Go and tell Dad I'm finished and he can put you in the bath."

Billie puts her pajamas on and pads downstairs. Her mother is stirring something on the stove that smells delicious.

"Yum!" says Billie. "What's for dinner?"

"Minestrone soup with garlic bread," her mom says, smiling. "But it's a little way off yet. You can play outside for a bit if you like and I'll call you when it's ready."

Billie opens the back door. She stands on the back steps and looks out over the garden towards the big apple tree. The sun is setting and flickers of light **shimmer** through the leaves and **dance** across the grass. In a month or so the big green leaves will turn golden and fall to the ground.

Then the Secret Mystery Club's headquarters will no longer be hidden.

Gosh, it won't be the same then! Billie thinks. *Trees are very good at hiding things.*

Suddenly this gives her an idea. A super-duper idea! She dashes down the back steps and squeezes through the hole in the fence into Jack's garden. "Jack! Jack!" she yells. "I think I know where the ime-tay apsule-cay is hidden!"

Chapter Six

"We have to go now!" Billie begs.
"Come on! It's still light. We'll just
run to the school **quickly** and be back
before our parents even notice!"

Jack is sitting on the back deck
surrounded by a tiny city he
has made out of matchboxes.

He had just begun putting Lego people around his city when Billie came **bursting** through the side fence. Billie can see he is excited by her news, but he doesn't really want to go anywhere right now.

"But you're in your pajamas," Jack says, picking up a little house that has just fallen over. "Can't we just wait until tomorrow?"

Billie shakes her head. "No! I have a feeling Edwina knows something. If we don't hurry she might find the time capsule before us!

I'm sure it's in the old pepper tree somewhere," she says urgently. "Or buried underneath it. That tree would be as old as the school. It's the perfect place to hide something! I really have a good feeling about this. Come with me just quickly? Please? Pretty please?"

Jack looks towards the back door of his house, then at Billie again. He shakes his head. "We're having dinner soon, Billie."

Billie frowns. "You're no fun, Jack!" she says. "This could be our biggest discovery ever and you just want to sit here and play with your Lego? Well, fine. I'll go by myself then!"

She stomps away and then runs down the side of the house and into the street.

The sun has slipped a little bit lower and the sky is beginning to blush pink. *I'll only be ten minutes,* she thinks. *No one will even notice I'm gone.*

Billie runs to the school at the end of her street. When she reaches the school gate she pulls at it. It's locked. Billie hangs her head, feeling disappointed.

She knows that she should just go home and look tomorrow. But now she feels absolutely sure the time capsule is hidden in the tree somewhere. She can see the old pepper tree through the iron gate, standing like a big, **shaggy** monster in the middle of the playground.

Billie looks up at the gate. It is tall, but she is sure she could climb it. Does she **dare**?

As she is trying to decide, she hears a voice from behind her. "Hi, Billie."

Billie's heart leaps in her chest. She spins around. It's Edwina.

"What are you doing here?" Billie asks.

Edwina shrugs. "I told you. I can see the whole school from my bedroom window. I saw you try the gate, so I came to talk to you."

"What do you want?" Billie frowns. "Why do you keep following me?"

Edwina smiles mysteriously. "I know what you're looking for, Billie. And I can help you find it."

"What do you mean?" Billie splutters. She pretends she has no idea what Edwina is talking about, but her cheeks burn **hot**. "I'm not looking for anything."

"Oh well," Edwina says, turning away from Billie. "I guess you won't want to see what I have, then."

"Wait!" Billie calls out after her. "What is it?"

Edwina stops. "First, you have to tell me what you're looking for," she says. "Then, if I help you find it, you have to let me join your club."

Billie feels her heart start to beat faster. "What club? I don't know what you're talking about!" Her voice comes out high and squeaky.

Edwina pauses and smiles at Billie.

"You're not the only detectives in this school, you know." She turns around and walks away. "If you want the clue to uncover your mystery, come and find me."

Chapter Seven

Billie stands on the sidewalk, staring after Edwina. She knows she really should go home. She's not sure what time it is, but when she looks up at the sky she can see one, two, three pale stars have appeared. Billie is not allowed out after dark.

But it's not dark yet. Billie tells herself. *And I'll only be a few more minutes. I have to find out what Edwina knows! I can't go home now!*

She takes a big breath and runs after Edwina. She catches up just as Edwina reaches her front door.

"Wait!" she says. "We're looking for a time capsule. Mrs. Singh told us about it. But you have to promise not to tell anyone I told you. My friends would kill me!"

Edwina smiles. "I knew it! I heard you talking in Mrs. Singh's office."

"What? You were listening to us?" Billie says crossly.

Edwina **blushes** a little. "Only because I needed to, to solve the mystery," she says. "Sometimes detectives have to do that, right?"

Billie is still a bit cross, but Edwina has a point. After all, the SMC has had to listen at doors before, too!

"I have something in my bedroom that I think will help you find the time capsule," says Edwina. "Come with me!"

Billie follows her into her house. She can hear a TV playing loudly and someone talking at the end of the hallway. Edwina leads her into the first bedroom on the left. She points at her window. It has a clear view across to the school grounds.

"Wow! You can see everything from here!" Billie says, amazed.

"It's a good spot for spying," Edwina says **cheekily**. "I'm a spy as well as a detective."

"Me too!" says Billie. "Alex says they're not the same thing, but I think, *really*? What's the difference?"

"Right!" Edwina grins. Billie grins back.

Edwina opens a drawer in her desk and pulls out a rolled up piece of paper.

"What's that?" Billie asks.

"This," Edwina says **dramatically**, "is the clue you've been looking for."

Billie hovers next to Edwina as she unrolls the paper. "Is it a map?" Billie asks. "Of a building?"

"Not just any building," Edwina says. "The *school* building. This is a photocopy of the original plans. Look, it says here: 1923. The school is nearly a hundred years old. Can you believe it?"

"Wow!" Billie says. "That's older than my Nana. And she's old!" Then she frowns. "Mrs. Singh told us that the plans were lost ages ago, though. How did you find them?"

"My mom's an architect," Edwina says. "She was in charge of renovating the school before I was born. The plans must have been lost then, but luckily Mom found this copy when she was clearing out her office the other day. She thought I'd find them interesting.

And when I overheard Mrs. Singh telling you about the time capsule, I knew I had the perfect clue to help solve the mystery!"

While she is talking, Edwina unrolls the map across her desk. She and Billie lean over it, staring down at the pale lines on the page.

"That's the front entrance to the school," says Edwina, pointing. "And there's the main corridor."

Billie nods. She finds the map a bit hard to read.

The school on the map looks much smaller than it is now. But now that Edwina has pointed out the front entrance, she starts to recognize some of the other buildings.

"So that's the music room, right?" says Billie.

"Yep," says Edwina. "And that's the library."

"What's that, then?" Billie asks, pointing to a small empty space between the library and the music room on the map.

Edwina frowns. "Hmm. I don't know. It looks like a big cupboard, maybe. But there are bookshelves all along that wall in the library, and there's no door on that wall in the music room. I can't **believe** I didn't notice that before!"

The two girls look at each other, excited. Billie can tell they are both thinking the same thing.

The space looks like the perfect place to hide a time capsule!

Chapter Eight

Billie runs all the way home, her bare feet slapping the pavement. She is bubbling with excitement. A secret room hidden between two walls! What could be more thrilling? Billie can't imagine how her life could get any better.

But just as she arrives at her house, she sees something that makes her heart sink. Her dad is striding towards her with Jack by his side. Jack looks **worried** and a little apologetic. But Billie's dad just looks mad. Very mad!

"What do you think you're doing, Billie?" he says angrily.

"Oh! Sorry!" Billie says. It sounds silly, but there is nothing else she can think of to say.

"You didn't even tell us where you were going!" he continues. "You must never do that. Luckily Jack knew where you were."

Billie hangs her head. She knows what she did was very wrong. "I'm sorry," she says again, in a small voice.

Her dad **sighs** and pulls Billie into his arms. "We were really worried, Billie," he says. "You know you can't go out on your own at night."

"I wasn't thinking," she says quietly.

"Thanks, Jack," Billie's dad says. "You'd better get back to your dinner now." He walks Jack to his front door.

Billie is quiet all through dinner. She feels bad that she made her parents worry so much. Even Noah senses something is wrong. Usually he is noisy and chatty, but tonight he just pokes at his food with his fork.

He looks up at Billie and frowns. "Never do dat again, Billie!" he says crossly, wagging his finger at her.

Billie looks at her mom, who is trying not to laugh. She looks at her dad. He bites his smile and looks away. Then they all look back at Noah, who has put on his angriest face possible. At that moment all three of them burst into laughter.

"What?" says Noah, surprised. "What? Are you happy again, Momma?"

"Yes, Nozy, darling," Billie's mom says. "I'm happy again now."

She stands up and puts one arm around Noah and one around Billie and pulls them in tight.

"Thanks, Noah," Billie whispers. "You're the best." Noah still looks a little unsure about what he has done but smiles happily all the same.

Chapter
Nine

The next day is Sunday and Billie calls

an emergency meeting of the SMC

in their secret headquarters. The four

of them climb up into the tree house.

Billie's dad brings them hot chocolate

in mugs, and toasted raisin bread

with melted butter.

"Thank you!" everyone calls out.

Billie's dad waves as he walks back to the house to put Noah down for his morning nap.

"So, what's new, Billie?" Mika asks excitedly.

"Yeah, tell us!" says Jack. "Did you find anything at school last night? She was in so much trouble," Jack tells Alex and Mika.

Billie wriggles uncomfortably. "You don't have to rub it in!

Anyway, it was worth it. I think I've found the missing clue that will lead us to find the time capsule!"

"Really?" says Mika. "Wow! What did you find?"

"Well, it's not really me who found it," Billie says. "It's...um, Edwina, actually."

"The spy?" Alex says, frowning. "But that's **terrible** news!"

"No, no, she showed it to me," Billie says. "She could have taken it straight to Mrs. Singh, but she decided to show me instead."

"Why?" says Mika, narrowing her eyes suspiciously.

Billie feels her stomach tightening. She is worried her friends aren't going to like what she has to say next. "She wants to be a member of our club," she says **nervously**.

The other three glance at each other with frowns on their faces.

"Hmmm…" says Jack eventually, looking unsure.

"I thought we decided it would only be the four of us," says Alex.

"I know what we agreed," Billie says. "But Edwina has a map! A copy of a hundred-year-old map of the school when it was first built. And listen to this: there is a secret room inside the school. Hidden between the library and the music room. That's where I reckon the time capsule will be hidden."

Mika gasps. "A secret room?"

Billie nods.

"How do we know the map's not a fake?" Alex says, crossing his arms.

"Maybe Edwina just drew it herself so she could join our club?"

Billie holds back her smile. "Well, there's only one way to find out! We check it out tomorrow!" she says. "But if the map leads us to find the time capsule, it's only fair that Edwina gets to join the SMC. After all, she has already shown what a good detective she is! Deal?"

Alex looks at Jack. Jack looks at Mika. Mika looks at Billie. Then they all smile and stick their hands out. "Deal!" they all say together.

Then they all crow loudly. "Ock-a-doodle-doo-cay!"

The four of them meet at the school library as soon as it opens on Monday morning. Miss Davenport is surprised to see them hovering at the door. "My goodness," she says. "What are you four doing here so early? Is there anything I can help with?"

"No, no, it's fine, thank you," Billie says quickly. "We're just researching a project, that's all."

Then she waits until Miss
Davenport is busy at her desk again
before leading the others over to
the far wall, which backs onto
the music room. The whole wall
is hidden by bookshelves. Billie
reaches towards a row of books in
the middle and begins to pull them
out, one by one.

"What are you doing?" asks Jack
anxiously, swinging his head
around to see if Miss Davenport
has spotted them.

"Stand in front of me so she can't see!" says Billie.

Soon there is a pile of books on the floor and a big gap in the bookshelf. Billie reaches her hand inside and runs her fingers along the smooth back wall. At first she feels nothing. She pulls out a couple more big books and slides her hand along farther. Then she feels something. A little bump in the wall.

"I think I've found something!" Billie squeals. "It could be the entrance to the secret room!"

"Let's go and tell Mrs. Singh," Alex says, helping Billie shove all the books back onto the shelves.

"Not yet," Billie tells him. "There's no way she'll agree to cutting a hole in the wall without proof that there is something behind here."

Jack looks at Billie like he knows what she is going to say next. "And to prove it, we need…" he begins.

Billie smiles. "…the fifth member of the SMC," she finishes.

"I guess a deal is a deal, right?" says Mika, smiling back.

"Right," says Billie.

Chapter Ten

Billie, Jack, Alex and Mika wait for Edwina at the front gate. When she arrives, she looks surprised to see them all waiting for her.

"You were right!" Billie says, excited. "We found something behind the bookshelves in the library.

It feels like it could be a sealed-up doorway!"

"Alex didn't believe the map you showed Billie was real," Mika adds. "But it must be!"

Alex blushes. "Yeah. Sorry, I didn't believe you," he mumbles, kicking at the concrete beneath his feet. "I thought maybe you'd just drawn it yourself. You know, so you could join our club."

"Wow!" says Edwina, looking **surprised**.

"But we'd love you to join our club now!" Billie grins. "We all think you're a pretty good detective."

"And spy!" Jack adds, grinning. "I can't believe you were spying on us the whole time Billie was teaching us pig Latin. You must be good at sneaking around."

"So, we'd be honored to have you," Billie says in a formal voice. "Can you get your map so we can show Mrs. Singh what we found?

It's the only way we'll be able to convince her to open up the wall to see what's behind there."

"Um, sure!" says Edwina, still with a look of surprise on her face. "I'll run back home and get it now." She turns to go back across the street, but then pauses, and spins around again. Now she has a huge smile on her face. "And… anks-thay, Illie-bay!"

Billie laughs. "O-nay oblem-pray."

Within a few minutes, the original members of the SMC, along with their newest member, are sitting in Mrs. Singh's office. They are **jiggling** with excitement. Mrs. Singh is studying the map of the school on her desk.

"Well, my goodness gracious me!" she says, looking up at them and pushing her reading glasses up onto her head.

Billie has never seen Mrs. Singh look so excited.

"You know, I think you might be right! It does look like there's a little room there. That's certainly worth investigating! What a **clever** group of detectives you are!"

"We couldn't have done it without Edwina," Billie says quickly.

"Well, once again you have shown how well you work together as a team," Mrs. Singh says, smiling. "And it looks like Edwina will make a valuable member of your club!"

Billie glances at Edwina, who looks proud. "Elcome-way!" she whispers.

"Ank-thay ou-yay!" Edwina whispers back. Billie can see the tips of her ears have turned pink underneath her hair.

"We might have to close the library for a couple of days," Mrs. Singh says. "But I think it's about time that time capsule was found, don't you? I can't wait to see what's in it! And I think our local media might be pretty interested, too.

I'll give them a call." Then she pauses, looking thoughtful. "There is one problem, though."

"What's that?" Billie asks, feeling a flutter of worry in her stomach. She hopes they haven't done anything wrong. Mrs. Singh looks suddenly very serious.

Then Mrs. Singh's face breaks into a huge smile. "I'm afraid your Secret Mystery Club might not remain secret for much longer.

Once the word gets out who discovered the **treasures** in the school walls, you kids will be famous!"

Billie and her friends squeal and dance up and down on the spot. Famous? This is the best news ever.

Chapter Eleven

That weekend, the Secret Mystery Club have an extra-special club meeting at Billie's house. But instead of meeting in the tree house, this time they are all in Billie's family room, gathered around the TV.

Everyone's parents are here, too. They are all crowded into the room, sitting on the couches and on the floor, chatting loudly.

Billie's dad has baked chocolate cupcakes especially for the occasion, with the letters SMC across the tops in green icing.

Noah has already eaten three of their special cupcakes and has left sticky chocolate fingerprints all over the coffee table.

He climbs onto Billie's lap to make sure he is right in the middle of the fun. Billie rubs off the chocolate he has smeared on her jeans.

"Hi, Ina!" Noah says, waving to Edwina. No matter how many times Billie tells Noah her name, he still can't say it right. She has given up trying to teach him.

"Here it is!" Billie's mom says, **dashing** over to the TV to turn the sound up. "Shhh, everyone!"

They all fall quiet and stare at the TV. Everyone cheers when an image of their school comes up on the screen. They watch the reporter speak into a microphone.

"For nearly a hundred years, this school has hidden a long-lost secret deep within its walls. A secret message from the students of the past to students of today. The whereabouts of this time capsule had long been forgotten, and it took five intrepid young detectives to uncover the treasure."

Everyone cheers loudly again. Especially the five members of the SMC!

"Look, look!" Mika shouts. "It's Mrs. Singh!"

The reporter holds the microphone up to Mrs. Singh, who blinks nervously into the camera. "Yes, well, I've always known there was a time capsule hidden in the school," she says, "but it had become a bit of an urban myth, handed down from one school principal to another.

I never dreamed ours would be the lucky generation to find it."

Now the camera shows the library. Even though the area has been roped off, Billie catches glimpses of people she knows **jumping** and **waving**, trying to get on TV.

She giggles. "Look! There's Benny and Sam! And is that Rebecca there?"

They all laugh when the camera catches a shot of Miss Davenport looking annoyed that her once neat library is such a terrible mess.

Finally, the camera focuses on what they've been waiting for. Once Billie had pointed out the seam in the wall behind the bookshelves it had been easy for builders to carefully cut out a square of the wall. Behind it, just as they'd hoped, was a large metal chest tucked away in the little gap between the two rooms.

Everyone in Billie's family room watches, holding their breath, as the camera zooms in on the chest.

The mayor has been invited for the occasion. She makes a speech about what a wonderful day this is. Then she opens the chest **carefully**.

Two experts from the museum reach into it with white gloves and pull out the things inside, one by one.

"Here we have a box of old pen nibs," one expert says, holding one up for the viewers to see. "And here is an inkwell. And this is called a slate," he continues, pointing to what looks like a small blackboard.

"Children wrote on these with slate pencils to save paper."

"Like olden-day iPads," the other expert jokes. Everyone laughs.

The experts continue to pull out things from the box and explain how each item was used at school a hundred years ago.

"It's incredible how well preserved everything is," says one expert. "This is really quite a find!"

Finally, one of them pulls out a small bundle of letters.

She gently unties the ribbon around them and reads aloud the first letter of the bundle:

To the children of the future,

We hope that whenever you find this time capsule, years from now, you will get a glimpse of what life was like in our day.

We have written stories and drawn pictures of what we think your life looks like in the future. We hope you enjoy them.

Signed,

Mr. T. Barton and schoolchildren

"He was the principal at the school when it first opened," Billie's dad explains to the others.

The expert carefully unfolds some of the drawings and holds them up to the camera. Some of them are very funny.

"Look! They thought we would be traveling around in flying cars!" Alex laughs.

"And is that an alien sitting in the classroom?" Mika giggles.

"Well, I'm sure they couldn't have imagined that we would be watching this on TV!" Edwina's mom says. "The world was a very different place back then."

The expert gently places the bundle of letters back into the box. Then she promises that they will organize an exhibition of all its contents at the museum. "Meanwhile," she says, "we want to thank the five clever children who uncovered this treasure. Would you five please step forward?"

The camera pans over all the excited kids in Billie's school, waving and jumping around. Finally, it rests on the five nervous faces of Billie and her friends as they walk towards the mayor.

"Three cheers for the Secret Mystery Club!" Billie's dad calls out, as on screen, Billie shakes hands with the mayor. Everyone joins in. **"Hip, hip, hooray! Hip, hip, hooray! Hip, hip, hooray!"**

"Well, we can't really call it the Secret Mystery Club now," Alex says.

"True," Billie says. "We're definitely not a secret anymore. Everybody knows about us now."

"Just when I've joined, too!" Edwina says, looking a bit sad.

"Don't worry," Billie says, smiling mysteriously. "I'm sure I'll come up with something else – just as fun!"

The End